Night Flying navigates darkness using only the instruments of the author's finely tuned imagination. The work defies classification—poem, novella, epistolary meditation—while engaging many literary modes and amply fulfilling Ezra Pound's famous dictum, *Make it new.*

Audacious and original, it fuses Job-like questioning of God's goodness with the colloquial exchange of emails, touching, as it does so, upon religious heritage, the flawed human flesh, childhood hopes, death's certainty, the limits of language and truths to be apprehended only in silence. At the same time, the work embodies a powerful dialogue between the certainties of tradition and the dislocations of post-modernism, which in no way obscures its simpler and grander purpose.

Night Flying is, above all else, a touching evocation of physical and spiritual suffering and love.

—**Tony Connor**, poet, playwright, and Fellow of the Royal Society of Literature. His books of poetry include *The Empty Air* and *Things Unsaid* (Anvil Press, London).

NIGHT FLYING

Joy Christine Mlozanowski

kin press

SECOND EDITION

Cover & book design by E.S.M.
© Kin Press

ISBN: 978-0-9989293-7-8

Kin Press
kinpress.org

NIGHT FLYING

March 27, Sunday

Dear God:

How long has it been since we
talked? Since I prayed?

Two dozen years, I think—
if I count back to that little girl

who begged you to please fix
her best friend, a boy born deaf.

That was me—a seven-year-old
who promised she'd give up

licorice jellybeans forever,
if you fixed your mistake.

I wanted him to hear me sing
Hallelujah Chorus just once.

Wearing my pink-ribboned
Easter hat, I knelt under

your stained-glass resurrection,
my mother's calm fingers

closing around my palm
while I bargained with you

for a miracle. She whispered,
Don't ask for that, Mae.

She said miracles are illusions,
like those bright stains of glass,

pieced together to make us believe—
and what we call a mistake

is a blessing we can't understand.
That's the day I quit praying,

stopped singing, began dreaming
of colors, of painting. I wanted

to create my own bright miracles,
not accept your mistakes.

Is it a mistake to pray now?
Now, I'm thirty-one and pregnant,

and bargaining for a blessing
I can understand.

I lie in the ocean of a dim, familiar room, white sheet
swirled around this rising mound of belly—my island of
fifteen weeks. Thomas sits at my side, his face afloat in
the ultrasonic glow.

Dr. Reed pilots her machine and we hold our breath like
we've already gone too deep, lungfuls from surfacing.
She can't find the tiny details we've come for.

Details we never believed would be missing.

No fingers, toes. No hands. No feet.

Dr. Reed looks up, a silhouette. Shakes her head. Tells
us, *I'm so sorry.*

I close my eyes, see a small brown cub curled in its
den—four soft paws, sleeping. A pastel sketch. A gift
from my best student.

We'll need an x-ray, she says. *It's good we found this early.*

Thomas touches me with his cool palm, tries to ground
me. He asks if *early* means she'll take care of it, as if
we're curing a disease. But I know the leaning in his
voice, can hear the way *take care of* sounds like *take away.*

And I know this is not an illusion.

Dr. Reed offers, *You'll want to talk this over. Talk with someone you trust.*

She doesn't know my mother has been dead fifteen years, and Father Simon will only tell me to pray.

He'll say every new life is a gift.

And I'll ask him, *If God doesn't make miracles, how can he answer any prayer?*

Tears bleeding
into silence between us—
I try to pray, hanging on.

March 29, Tuesday

Dr. Reed shows us the blue-black negative, shimmering,
points to tiny pearls. Clustered bones, places where
hands and feet will never grow.

Thomas sits across the room. Not moving. Not looking.

We should talk about options, she says. *Make decisions soon.*

I ask Dr. Reed for more time—tell her I've already
made plans to fly, visit home. Tell her how my
grandmother has been sick since Christmas.

Her warm hand finds my shoulder before she reaches to
click off the light-box. *It's okay to go.*

I stop her, want one more minute to look closer—*how
soon?*—to see the perfect head on its caterpillar spine.
That shell-edged profile of a tiny face. Ribs made to
cradle a beating heart.

As soon as you both can agree.

Thomas needs air, says he'll meet me outside.

Dear God, I don't tell her what you already know, what
I can't see. Another Easter is almost here and I want to
fly away—fly one thousand miles to find your answer.
Back to that safe place where I was born, not perfect.

Where I grew up beside the Iowa River, digging for smooth quartz, making wishes.

Where my friend Will once taught me his silent language.

And listened to every secret.

Last finger, first finger,
thumb extended—
I love you.

I don't even know if you're a girl or boy,
growing inside me—

worry about other parts of you,
still unseen, that might not be whole.

I'd tell you a story, if I could—
how when I was six years old

I stood at the edge of the river,
knee-deep, holding my net.

Fish darted, circled, catching light—
water rippled. In one scoop,

I caught a quick of silver.
On the riverbank, I untangled

my small, glistening catch, tried
to hold that silver in my hands—

felt it slip, watched it fall
between dry stones. I knew

it wished only to swim again,
breathe. Afraid, I reached down—

beyond wanting to run home,
beyond my knotted heart,

beyond death. I threw my net away.
You are my shiny fish now,

circling beneath this surface—
rippling water. If I could

hold you, I would ask
who you are, what you want.

I'd find the water, let you go—
let you swim home.

Dear God:

When Thomas comes home
from his workday of decisiveness,
of giving orders,
he moves through the house

like he's lost.
We're both lost.
All sense of our direction
shows in the trench of his brow.

He prays in small explosions.
How could this happen?
This can't be happening—
not to us.

Dear God:

I don't ask for new prayers.
Father Simon gives them to me anyway.

He tells me, *God will show you the answer.*
He says, *Prayer helps us do the right thing.*

But he doesn't know how your absence blinds me.
He doesn't know the only thing I pray for

is an answer that will silence Thomas—
his helpless conviction. *We can't do this.*

April 4, Monday

His hands find me in the night,
those hands I've loved,

those fingers that used to know
the skin I live in. But his touch

speaks its own language now,
tries to convince me of its own need—

to hold what's familiar, safe.
I smell the salt-sweet of Thomas's hair

while he whispers in the dark.
I want a child, too. But not like this.

I miss our life before *this*—
miss the unspoken assumptions

that once shaped us, made us fit.
He says he's glad I'll have a few days

away from him to think about *this*.
Then he asks if I ever pray

and if I believe God ever answers.
I lie—tell him I try to hear the river

when I pray, like home still moving
through me. And I wonder if three days

in Iowa will change anything.
Maybe this time next Sunday,

I'll be back here in Westerly, back
in this bed next to him, whispering—

this time, not sure where home is,
but with a blessing alive inside me.

Dear God:

I can't sleep.
I leave Thomas to fight alone in his dreams.

My hands work in the computer's glow,
filling search boxes—
typing and retyping the words Dr. Reed gave us.

Amanous: having no hands.
Apodal: having no feet.

But my search only conjures what I've already seen.

It doesn't show me a reason for what's missing.
It doesn't tell me what else might be wrong.

I stumble through sites honoring children
with false limbs, missing organs—
blind, deaf, paralyzed.

Loved, they are all survivors.

A moth spins around my lamplight—
flits like the ghost moth Will once jarred for me
when we were twelve.

The night he promised we'd stay friends, no matter what.
I sketched its wings before letting it go.

Maybe I've forgotten how to sing,
but I can still draw the illusion of night flying.

And maybe you, Absent God,
can give me a sign you're listening.

Dear Will:

I know I haven't written in a while,
not since you sent that card four Christmases ago—
the one with the Three Wise Men
that got lost in the mail, and didn't show up until spring.

I've been wondering how you are.

I'm flying out to see my grandmother,
and I know this is short notice—
but can I see you this Saturday?

—Mae

April 6, Wednesday

Dear Mae:

It's good to hear from you, a surprise in my nightly routine, checking email before sleep.

But tonight, I'm still awake, thinking I should know what to say, wanting to tell you that the years and miles have never mattered between us. And my hands would rather show you these words in sign, not have to shape them through this keyboard, letter by letter.

I think seeing you this Saturday would be perfect.

But for now, I'll just tell you that I'm never far from our river, where we used to dig in the shallows for wishing stones. When I drive south out of Garner the river follows me, nearly all the way to the airstrip in Clarion. My father's Piper Cherokee is there, still waiting to fly again.

And I still wonder what your voice sounded like, echoing up the banks.

—Will

April 8, Friday

Dear God:

Tomorrow is the day I'll see home.

Tomorrow we'll talk about everything I've missed since
leaving there—
everything I've missed
about that dark wide earth and tall bright sky.

But today, I'll just pray you can hear me.

I kneel alone—
fingers braided, begging,
toes and knees aching.

Dear God:

I asked him to stop in Garner at the river's edge
where we pushed our hands through the crust
of winter's thaw, numb and searching
for new quartz—
and I knew I'd never wish again, as much as this day,
that he could have heard us both
laughing.

I met her at noon—
but evening shadowed near,
too soon.

I saved her last, wordless touch.

Dear Will:

I'm back in Rhode Island already—can't believe that just this morning I woke up to a yawning Midwest sky. The violet canopy of clouds lifting to a clear yellow dawn.

Did yesterday really happen?

Before my flight, I visited Grandma Jean one more time, sat by her bed while she sipped tea, her eyes as bright as I've ever seen them. She's not afraid of dying.

She said, *Tell me more about how you've been, Mae. I've been missing you.*

I couldn't tell her about the baby, how scared I am— wouldn't want her to worry. So I told her I had seen you, told her that your father has cancer, too. She nodded, said she'd heard the news.

Then she asked, *What are you thinking, Love?*

I didn't confess how you've visited my dreams all these years. I didn't tell her that in my sleep, you and I are still two skinny kids playing by the river, all muddy hands and feet.

It's getting late and I have a hundred things I want to

write. Thomas is waiting for me to come to sleep. And here I am thinking about that last hour with your arm around me, parked on the edge of a snow-patched cornfield, watching the night rise into a starless sky.

We were warm and safe.

—Mae

Dear Mae:

I hope seeing you really happened, hope I wasn't stumbling through a dream, picking up rocks by the river.

I carried my wishing stone all day. But stones are deaf, like me—they can't hear what I wish, even if I tried wishing. They don't know I've learned to hear beyond signs. They don't know I feel your words, the same as touching a finger to your throat.

I dreamed last night of your hands. Tell me your dreams and I'll tell you what I've learned about miracles. Like my father coming home to die, my mother convinced he can still be cured. He signs his fears, and his secret wishes. Prays there's a God who's listening. Asks me to help him die without pain.

But I'm not ready to wish for anything. I won't pray.

Just know I'm here. I'll look for your messages every night.

Love, Will

Dear Will:

When my mother was dying, I made a wish every night that she wouldn't wake to a new morning of pain. That her breath would ease without struggle. Then at dawn, I'd wish I could keep her one more day.

I watched pain bury her soul, slowly.

I understand your mother's hope, not accepting that your father has come home to die. If she could, she'd root him like a new garden. Water his soul. Wish for a miracle.

I know wishing isn't a cure, but I don't know if I could have helped my mother die. I don't know if I could do what your father has asked of you. I can't even do what Thomas wants—can't pretend this child isn't part of me. Isn't whispering to me.

My stone from the river carries my worries.

It's time to sleep now. Midnight is here. A quarter moon.

—Mae

Pearl edge of God's finger—
cradle or sickle
in this black womb of sky?

Dear Mae:

Today, a different nurse came to see my father. She
brought a bottle of liquid morphine, showed us how to
put drops on his tongue.

My father watched her confident hands, smiled as if
relieved. My mother read the bottle-label and cried.

I don't know if I can help my father die.

I know my mother isn't ready for goodbyes.

Tonight I sat by his bed, read his thin fingers, signing.
They remind me of pale branches, stripped clean of
bark.

He tells me he still dreams of flying his Piper Cherokee,
chides me that I haven't kept my promise to become a
pilot, too. But I'm simply the mechanic he taught me to
be—the workings of piston and gear are what I know.

I say goodnight, loosen the bedcovers at his side.

My mother lies down next to him, their new ritual. She
stays until he sleeps, then shadows away to the bed they
shared for thirty-five years.

She arranges a place for him there, hopes he'll come to

her in the night—as if her invitation might bring a cure.

Maybe Thomas will hear the same whisper you hear.
Then you won't need your worry stone anymore.

Love, Will

Dear Will:

It's as though we've become stewards of these lives that don't belong to us. But still, they're part of what we breathe. I think God is being cruel when we're asked to decide. He leaves us so little time to choose.

Know that I'm here, too, and will listen.

Love, Mae

Doubt swallows all
comfort of sleep—
follows my soul into night.

Dear Mae:

Since my father's been home, I chase sleep. I miss the escape of night, of dreaming. I check on him every hour, lean close to feel his breath on my cheek.

Most nights, my mother sleeps. She dreams that tomorrow life will continue to hum forward, like the engines that oil my fingers every day. Every day, I'm fixing what's broken— fitting metal to metal to make machines fly again.

If we don't have a choice to live, shouldn't we at least have a choice to die?

I'm here, no matter what you choose.

Love, Will

April 14, Thursday

Dear Will:

Lingering in the driveway, leaning into my car,
Thomas says, *It's just a word. Abortion.*

Under a gray dawn, low-slung and heavy with snow,
he tells me, *It's only a procedure.*

He says, *It's like your flight getting canceled
after you've already boarded the plane.*

I want to pretend he's really talking about
a turn in the weather,
or when somebody finds a problem
with the wing.

But then he says, *There's always another plane.*

I ask, *So do you think a soul just climbs out,
finds a new body to fly in?*

He answers, *It makes sense, doesn't it?
Besides, what toys do you buy for a child with no hands?*

As if that had anything to do with flying.

I could scream until my lungs bleed.
But I'm late for work.

He doesn't know we're all born without something—
we're all flying to a place we can't see.

Love, Mae

Dear Mae:

I wish my words could be a cure that heals without pain.
Not like the chemo that's kept my father alive.

I'd be a medicine that soothes without numbing. Not
like the morphine that now helps him die.

He's the pilot, getting ready for his journey. When my
mother leaves us, he gestures for more drops on his
tongue. And I give them. Morphine chased by two sips
of water.

How many days until the liquid slows his breath and
stops his heart?

Even if I can't hear him whisper in his dreams, I can
read his signs. His hands tell me he's looking for that
curve of God's horizon, and he'll fly as far as the Piper
Cherokee can take him.

He reminds me that you only need a clear sky, a bright
line of horizon to guide you.

If I were a pilot, I'd help you climb through your clouds,
see that blue dome of sky.

I'd help you find your answers, shining.

But I'm just a doctor of flying machines. And maybe it's true—maybe we're all flying blind.

Love, Will

Dear Will:

I'm still awake.

I don't want to lie down next to Thomas, don't want to
think about choices, don't want to be grounded
to this life.

It's not that he doesn't love me—he just doesn't know
how he can ever love this child.

Every night he asks me why I won't do the thing
I can't do. Every night, his voice rises against mine, fists
clenching. Our lives broken by this dance, how can we
hide our tears?

I'm not sure whether he's afraid of my choice, or his
own.

Love, Mae

Dear Will:

It's raining here now, freezing—the trees will be glazed, heavy by morning.

You must be tired. How is your father today?

Sometimes dying can be more work than living, even if you're ready. But then I see how the trees hang on every autumn—they lose all fire and wait, black and naked, through another winter.

How do they know spring will ever come back?

I'm done with winter, this waiting.

Love, Mae

Dear Mae:

You ask about my father—but I just want to ask, how are you? I worry. Don't let Thomas's fear consume your hope.

My mother and I were up at 5:00 this morning, watching the sky brighten while my father slept. She told me a story about when I was born, her tired fingers speaking slowly. My father was afraid to hold me when the doctors told them I was deaf—didn't know if he could love a child who would never hear his voice, who would never speak like he did.

Then he realized I'd never even hear my own voice, knew he had to learn a new language.

Sometimes, we learn to love what's imperfect.

Love, Will

My body loves you.
It holds you.

I want all the doctors
and all their tests to be wrong.

I want to imagine your toes
on cool grass, in clear water—

your fingers finding warm earth
and smooth stones.

In church today, I talked to God
about everything—

about you and your father,
and about Grandma Jean.

About Will and his dying father,
his mother holding on.

I'm learning mothers do that—
it's in our cells.

I can't let you go.
You float inside me

while I search for remedies,
look for that place I'll land

and find reassurance—
or at least hope.

Then I can sleep at night.
Then I can stop blaming myself—

I must have done something wrong—
start feeling whole.

Dear God:

Father Simon tells me to trust you.
He says, *God always answers*—

you just have to watch, listen.
But still, I can't hear you

and maybe the only real sign
is the string of words that unravel

from Thomas's mouth every night,
the only words he gives me now—

You don't care what happens to us.
But it's already happened.

His *I love you*'s are gone.
He says he'll leave me.

He's already buried the life you've given us—
a child not even born.

Is this your sign, dear God?

April 17, Sunday

Dear Mae:

This morning, I found a ghost moth in our garage, wondered how it came to live there. I know letting it go means letting it die—it's too soon, too early. I left it resting above the door switch, knowing it will die, either way.

I worry when there's no message from you.

Tonight my father promised my mother that he'd wait for her on the other side, signing every word so I could hear, too. Then he closed his eyes and traced her cheek with his pale and knowing fingers. She leaned in, smoothed back her tangled hair and kissed him. She didn't cry.

I hid my own tears.

I wonder if the ghost moth will survive. Wonder if my mother is starting to let go. Wonder where you are, what you're feeling.

Love, Will

Dear Will:

I'm up late again.

The moon's full—my bright companion, watching me while Thomas sleeps. Sometimes I can feel his despair tremble the bed. But he's so far away now. My arms aren't long enough to reach him, to steady us.

I hide my crying, too. I don't want to tell him what I've decided. I don't know if he'll learn this language, to love what's imperfect.

Do you remember that time you caught a ghost moth for me, one summer night by the river? How I wanted to draw the patterns of its wings, so I could save them?

I wonder how a moth can fly in the darkness. How it knows which direction will bring it home.

Love, Mae

I kneel again—
cradle this womb, waiting,
hands folded in *Hail Mary*.

Dear Mae:

Another moth today.

Leaving work, I found it winging against the bulb above the wash sink—disoriented, lost. I scrubbed the day's oil from every grove of my fingers, from every crease of my palms. Then I cupped the moth and let him go, into the cold evening, unfolding.

It's the moon and the earth's pull that bring the moth home.

Tonight, my mother's waiting for me at the door, her hands telling me there's a change in my father—he's restless, asking for me. Her lips tight, she doesn't bother to say the words because there's no one else to hear. I can't remember the last time she smiled.

I wash my hands again, sit with my father. He touches his thumb to his boney chin, asks what my mother's doing, wants to know she's busy.

He tells me not to forget my promise, our secret.

I've always listened to what he told me to do, have to clamp down the grief inside me. But death isn't like putting a ratchet to a bolt. It's not like fixing a rotor assembly, or tuning an engine.

The bottle of morphine binds us. I give him the drops he
asks for, a precision move, like aligning the gears that make
machines fly. My mother walks in, sees the bottle in my
hand.

She tells me it's too soon to give more.

It's always too soon.

Love, Will

Dear God:

Sometimes I wonder if you care at all,
why you let my mother die in so much pain.

That was the way my father told it, bitterly.
But I was the one who stayed with her,

the same as Will sits with his father now,
watching over his death—hiding, helping.

Death is harder than being born.
We don't remember our arrival.

And we can only imagine our leaving.

Dear Will:

I know you can't tell your mother what your father has asked of you. But she must sense the time is close, staying near.

Are you alright? I think about your long nights, aching.

Today, I told Dr. Reed I want to keep this baby. Thomas bent forward, shook his head.

He covered his face as if someone had just told a horrible secret, a secret that changed everything he'd ever believed about his life. A secret that erased everything he ever imagined it should be.

But I'd already told him what I wanted. He already knows he's the father of a child he's not sure he can love. Dr. Reed asked if I was sure. Thomas left the room.

I said *yes*, and didn't cry.

Love, Mae

April 21, Thursday

Dear Mae:

The house is dark. My mother sits at my father's side, says
she smells a sweet change in his breath when he's sleeping.

A nurse was here all day. And tomorrow, Good Friday, I'll
stay home. I owe him this.

When I was a kid, I was convinced he'd never die. He'd take
me up in the Cherokee, ask me to co-pilot, and I'd pretend I
knew something about flying. I wanted to learn how all the
parts worked, what got it into the sky. I'd ask if I was
getting it right.

Now I watch his body, limbs tightening, fingers still trying
to tell me something. We've worked out a code. I sign
against his palm to ask if I'm getting it right. Two taps are
his answer back. Two taps mean yes.

I believe you're getting it right, too.

Love, Will

Maybe love is a direction
we choose—to give up
flying blindly.

April 21, Thursday

Dear Will:

My students are too young to know the luck of their perfect hands. They painted the bright colors of Easter today, dressed up plastic eggs in yellow, purple and green. One was a gift for me—a glittered egg with lavender stars, a tissue-paper chick inside.

When I come home to Thomas, the colors drain from my soul.

He thinks I've made the wrong decision, reminds me this is a choice we're supposed to make together. I remind him of his desperate silence, his threats to leave.

He tells me, *But people will feel sorry for us. They'll stare.*

I imagine a stranger's smile. A hello silenced by the thin wing of a baby's arm, reaching out.

He says, *What if something else is wrong, too—something we don't know yet?*

I confess it's a thought that scares me every day.

Then don't do this to us, he begs. *I can't do this.*

It's not only about you, I finally tell him. *And I'll do this alone, if I have to.*

I know it's really about us. I watch his mouth take a shape
I've never seen before. It's not about a child I know we're
destined to meet.

Love, Mae

April 22, Friday

Dear Mae:

More family has arrived—my father's brother and sister stay close now, too.

I've tucked my wishing stone under his pillow, keep the bottle of morphine in my pocket. My mother sits with my father, wetting his mouth, leaning to him. She hasn't had time to notice it's missing.

I wait in the doorway. There are murmurs I can't hear, so I watch—lips and eyes and hands. I read them, eavesdrop. My aunt signs and asks how I'm doing, tries to tell me what my mother whispers to my father.

And I think about that ghost moth I set free, able to fly somewhere for the few short days of its life.

Love, Will

Dear Will:

Do you think a soul can slip from one body into another,
like Thomas said?

Even if it can, I believe your father will always be near you.

Love, Mae

April 23, Saturday

Dear Mae:

My father is gone.

I slept on the couch outside his door, my mother with him for those last moments.

The morphine stayed in my pocket, while his lungs kept trying to pull air. Did I let him down? There's no logic to this. Not the way each part of a machine has its job in the workings of the whole.

What was the part I played, with my silence, my deafness? My hands that brought the liquid sleep he asked for, again and again, and again?

My mother closed his half-open eyes, spirit gone. She asked us to wait, not call anyone. I helped her wash his face and hands, slowly, unbend the limbs that were no longer stiff. We tucked fresh sheets around him, unfolded a blue quilt, and she lay back down for one more goodbye. His body took the surge of her tears.

Only my pounding heart reminds me that I'm still alive.

I wish I knew where the spirit flies to.

Love, Will

April 23, Saturday

Dear Will:

I lay down with my mother, too, when she died. Inside the dark ocean of a hospital room, I drifted with her, wrapped myself in damp sheets and the smell of her struggle.

I wish we could know the other side. That we could know whether we are still connected to each other in death, without the barrier of the bodies we live in. Then I realize I'm closer to this child I carry than I might ever be again.

I've buried my wishing stone in the garden, in a place where the nettle grows, where I've seen ghost moths rise in summer.

I'd fly back to see you, if I could.

Love, Mae

Cocoon now shed,
instinct takes wing—
unfolds toward home.

April 24, Sunday

Dear God:

Today is your Easter. Today, I will sit under your
stained-glass resurrection, and sing again—finally sing

in a church that's far away from the church
I prayed in when I was only seven.

I haven't figured out mistakes or blessings.
I don't understand miracles or illusions.

Father Simon doesn't have answers.
He just keeps telling me, *Pray. Have faith.*

I don't know why a deaf boy grows up
with a father who must learn to love him—

a father who'll one day ask his son
to help him die. Is that faith?

I don't know why you let my mother suffer
or why you've given me a child

without hands and feet, and a husband
whose anger smothers all hope.

Today is your Easter, so I'll sing—
praise your cruel glory, Dear God.

Dear Mae:

We visited the funeral director this evening, began making plans. He didn't mind that it's Easter. He knows death comes at inconvenient times.

My mother insists on burial, even though my father wanted cremation, to have his ashes released to the sky. I don't argue. If his body is preserved and boxed, grounded to the earth, at least it will be a place she can always find him.

She needs to keep him near.

At home, we look for the gray suit he saved for special occasions. And dig through old photos, trying to pick one for the obituary. We find my mother in her wedding dress, both arms wrapped around my father's neck, dancing, laughing.

She hangs on, eyes closed.

And there is my father holding me at two years old. My legs tucked inside his flight jacket, the Cherokee behind us. At the moment my mother clicks the shutter, he signs—first finger, last finger, thumb—a blurry, silent *I love you.*

I keep that picture, and the one she took of you and me by the river when we were six. You hold your fishing net above the water, that one you gave up by the end of summer.

I'm muddy and knee-deep, reaching for your hand,
smiling—knowing you'll reach back, take mine.

Love, Will

April 25, Monday

Dear Will:

I hope you are finding peace, somehow.

I confess I made a wish one Easter, wished that God would make a miracle, and fix you. A selfish request—I only wanted you to hear me sing. But my mother told me there's nothing to fix, that God doesn't make mistakes.

I still want to believe in miracles.

I love you.

—Mae

Dear Mae:

It was my wish, too. To hear your voice. To hear you, singing.

Love, Will

April 26, Tuesday

Dear Will:

I wish I could be with you tomorrow.

I called my Grandma Jean this morning, told her about your father. At first, she didn't know my voice, and I ached to hold her warm hands again, to sit with her and talk about everything this time. About the baby. About you.

She told me she loved me, and wished you and your family *Godspeed*. She said, *Keep them in your prayers*. And in her voice, I could hear my own hope coming back, more alive than ever.

Love, Mae

Dear Mae:

He would have liked the spot my mother chose.

A cold wind kept rising up the hill, shook the dark roses on his casket, made us all tremble as we stood around him under a white April sun.

I couldn't read the minister's lips, tried to whisper my own kind of prayer. My mother squeezed my arm, asked if I blamed her for burying him. She confessed she knew what he'd asked me to do, said she'd forgiven me.

But I told her there's nothing to forgive. *I only did what he wanted.*

She said, *All he wanted was to teach you to fly.*

But he's buried now. And I would fly to you, if I could.

Love, Will

Dear Will:

I thought of you all day.

Last night, I dreamed a ghost moth emerged from my womb and unfolded its perfect wings. I woke up alone, not afraid, not guessing anymore.

Thomas paced through the dark of our sleeping house. He's leaving tomorrow. I'm done with this anger that's exhausted us, the selfish words that have broken what we were. I pray he'll wake up and find his own blessing, choose the direction that will make him happy.

The moon is waxing tonight. I'll dream under its faint glow, imagine my own night flying.

Love, Mae

Thread of moonlight
weaves illusion—
until every spirit flies.

Dear God:

I just want to live in this one moment,
knowing you are somewhere,

maybe listening, maybe turning destiny—
God, keep this child flying with me.

ABOUT THE AUTHOR

Joy Christine Mlozanowski is a writer and visual artist who is drawn to the intersection of text and art, especially works relating to faith, nature, and the human body. By day, she is also a transpersonal therapist, patient advocate and wellness researcher-educator—by night, she follows her muse. You can connect with Joy at affinityworks.org.

* 9 7 8 0 9 9 8 9 2 9 3 7 8 *